Happy 1st Christmas Max!

Love Uncle Tim, Auntie Melissa, Odin, Deacon, Peaches and Stella

One day a little boy awoke,
sat up and rubbed his eyes,
looked over at his bedroom door,
and got a **big surprise**!

His name,
which he had stuck there,
had **vanished**, flown away!
"What exactly am I called?"
he wondered in dismay.

He searched inside his closet,
he peered in all his drawers,
he had a look beneath his bed,
crouched down on all fours.

What's this?
A magic rainbow trail!
It wasn't there before.
Could that be where his name had gone?
And did he dare explore?

The boy crept down the winding trail,
looking all around,
surrounded by fantastic sights,
astonished, and **spellbound**.

But finding a **lost name** is hard,
and takes great **bravery**.
How would the little boy get on?
Let's turn the page, and see!

In a jungle sat a **Monkey**,
muttering and grumbling –
the boy, even from far away,
could hear its tummy rumbling!

"Oh, woe is me," the Monkey cried,
"I'm absolutely famished!"
"**I've** lost my name," the boy replied.
"It's **completely** vanished."

Around the Monkey yellow fruit
was hanging by the bunch.
"I'd help you find your name," it said,
"but first **I need some lunch**."

"How about **bananas**?"
said the boy, "Just take your pick."
"Bananas? Ewww!" the Monkey said.
"They make me feel **quite sick**.

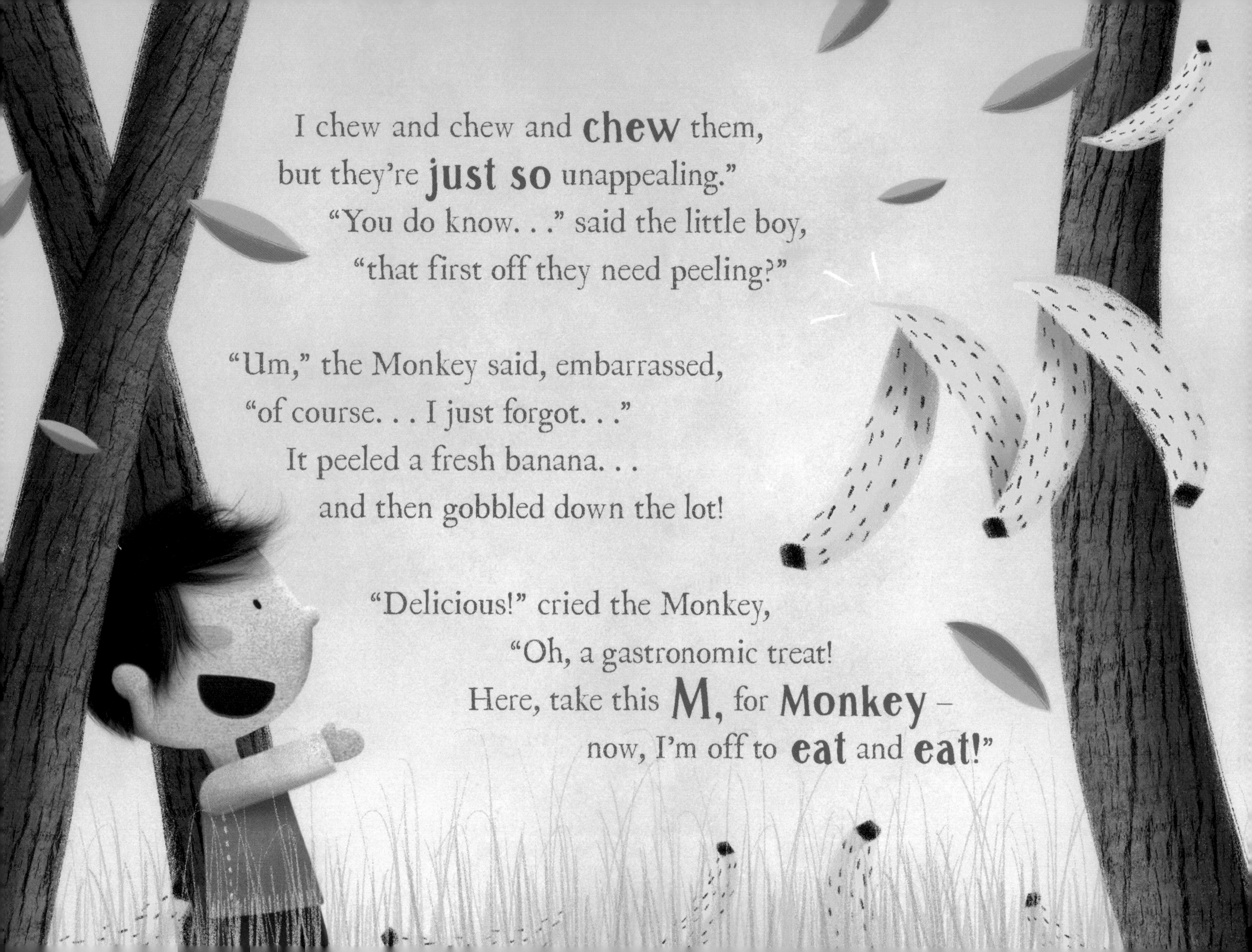

I chew and chew and **chew** them,
but they're **just so** unappealing."
"You do know. . ." said the little boy,
"that first off they need peeling?"

"Um," the Monkey said, embarrassed,
"of course. . . I just forgot. . ."
It peeled a fresh banana. . .
and then gobbled down the lot!

"Delicious!" cried the Monkey,
"Oh, a gastronomic treat!
Here, take this **M**, for **Monkey** –
now, I'm off to **eat** and **eat**!"

The little boy walked on and on, here, there and roundabout,
and came across an animal with a **tremendous** snout.

"Hello there," said the little boy,
"what animal are you?"
"I'm an **Aardvark**," said the beast,
"good morning! How'd you do?"

"Not so good," the boy replied,
"you see, I've lost my name."
"**Goodness me!**" the Aardvark cried,
"Now there's a **dreadful** shame!"

The Aardvark rooted busily,
"I need to find some lunch . . .
And if you're hungry too,
then I've got tasty **ants** to munch!"

"**Ants?**" the boy said, horrified, "No, really, **not for me!**"
And sat down, quite as gloomy as a little boy could be.

"Lost your name?" the Aardvark snuffled. "Well now, that won't do.
You mustn't give up yet though, and just sit there feeling blue.

Aardvark starts with two As –
I can surely spare you one.
I'm sure you'll come across your name
before the day is done."

"**Avast!**" a hairy Pirate cried,
"You've lost your name, you say?
That's not a tale a salty sea dog
hears of every day!

The name is
Captain Jack, my boy,
and I'll be frank with you –
I've got this treasure map,
but, well. . .
**I think that
I'm lost too!**"

The boy looked at the Pirate's map, then turned it right around.
"It's upside down, you silly, look! Here's where your treasure's found!"

"**Yo-ho!**" cried Captain Jack,
and straight away began to dig.
He soon pulled out a treasure chest,
then danced a happy jig.

"**Rich! I'm rich!**" he cackled,
"And it's thanks to you, it's true.
To show you that I'm grateful
I'll do **something nice
for you!**"

He took the map and tore a little piece, out of the middle.
“Here’s the **X** that marked the spot, to get you out your fiddle.”
And with that Captain Jack hurrahed, and whirled about in glee,
quite the jolliest Pirate who had ever sailed the sea!

The boy came by a **Wizard**, with a beard down to his knees.
"Lost your name?" he asked the boy, "Why let me help you, please!
Kazam," he cried, impressively,
"**kazoom! Az-a-ma-doo!**
And, just for good measure – why not? –
Abracadabra, too!"

A puff of smoke appeared, and then
a **searing flash of light**. . .
And suddenly
the Wizard shrank –
to only half his height!

"**Fiddlesticks!**" he cried,
"Oh, I'm the feeblest Wizard **ever!**
How often does my magic work?
Don't know? I'll tell you – **never!**"

He crossly snapped his wand in half, and threw it far away.
"That's it! I'll retrain as a plumber, starting now, today!

But I'd really love to help,
before I disappear. . .
My magic didn't work,
but I've got something for you here.

Take this W, for Wizard,
from my silly hat.
I'll never need it as a plumber,
I'm quite sure of that!"

An **Eagle** passed to say "Good morning," swooping from the skies.
"Hop on," he said, "we'll find your name – I'll use my **Eagle** eyes!"

"**Woo-hoo!**" the boy yelled happily,
the ground far, far below.
"**Hold on tight**," the Eagle cried.
"Remember, **don't let go!**"

They saw cows as small as ants,
and winding streams like silver bands,
a huge lake like a tiny puddle –
all the sights in the land.

"Spy your name?" the Eagle asked him, soaring here and there.
"No," the boy said sadly, "I can't see it anywhere."

"Don't give up," the Eagle said, – "**I'm King of all the Skies**,
which makes you **Prince** – why, that's so grand! Come on now, dry your eyes.

Look," he said, "down there, you see? Hanging in that tree!"
Yes! Something glinted miles below – **whatever could it be?**

Down they swooped and found an **E**, dangling bright and new.
"For **Eagle** – take it, for your name!" And with that, off he flew.

The boy climbed over jagged rocks, and got an awful scare –
he nearly wandered straight into a deep, dark Lion's lair!
Too late! The Lion spotted him, and cried out with a roar,
"Who are you? And just what are you doing at my door?"

"I d-don't know," the boy replied, "y-you see I've lost my name."
"Oh don't panic," said the Lion, "I'm really rather tame.

See, I'm in charge around these parts – I guess I'm like the **King**.
Which is great and stuff, I s'pose. . . but see now, **here's the thing**.

All the other animals do anything I say –
but they're so terrified of me, they never come and play."

"I'll play with you," the boy replied, "I'll show them how it's done."
And play they did, all morning – oh, the Lion **had such fun!**

The Lion gave the boy a medal,
once they'd played their game.
"It's an **L**, for **Lion** –
it will help to find your name!"

By the shore, a spiny **Lobster**
sulked in a rock pool.
"**What's the matter?**" asked the boy.
"Things," it said, "aren't cool.

I want to be a pianist,
play jazz in funky bands. . .
But piano playing's **tricky**,
when you've got **two claws** for hands.

All my friends play," it explained,
"the Shrimp's on **saxophone**.
The Shark's on **double bass**,
the Seahorse plays a mean **trombone**.

Anyway," it said, "that's my deal.
What brings you this way?"
"I've lost my name," the boy said,
"but I know what you can play!

You're right, to play piano
you need fingers and thumbs. . .
With those claws, you might do better
playing on the **drums**."

"Drums?" the Lobster said, surprised.
"Yeah, I could hold the sticks!
Keep that rhythm jumping. . .
That's how Lobsters get their kicks!"

It laughed and snapped its claws in glee,
then said, "before I split,
Take this **L** for **Lobster**. . .
I've got skins I need to hit!"

The little boy turned round
and headed back the way he'd come,
past all the **wondrous** things he'd seen,
and all the things he'd done.

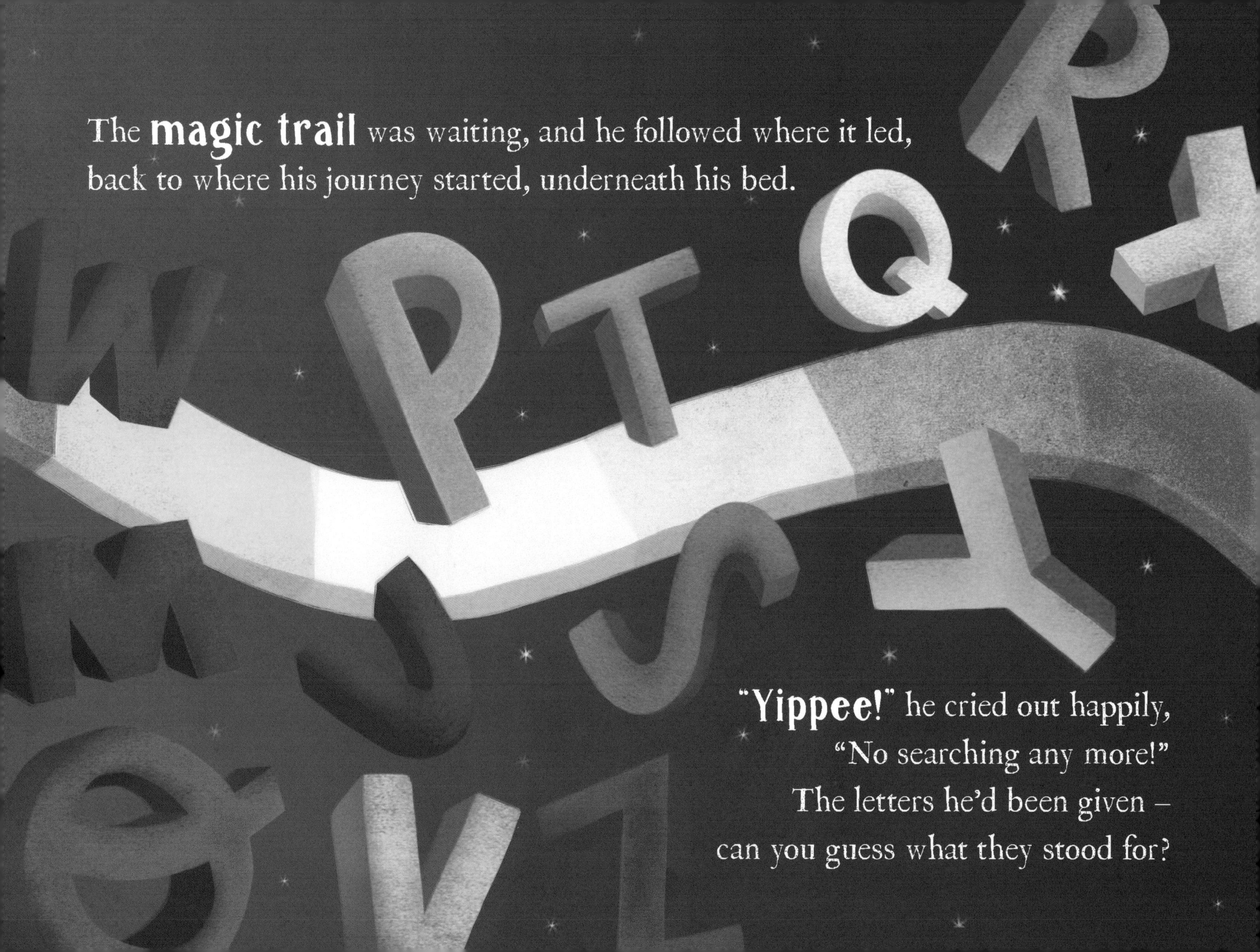

The **magic trail** was waiting, and he followed where it led,
back to where his journey started, underneath his bed.

"**Yippee!**" he cried out happily,
"No searching any more!"
The letters he'd been given –
can you guess what they stood for?

He felt so tired and weary,
and yet also full of joy,
what a quite **amazingly**
courageous little boy –
called . . .

MAXWELL

Ready for another adventure?

How about a cosmic journey all the way to
the best place in the galaxy. Home!
(Includes an actual satellite image of your child's home!)

Create their book at
www.lostmy.name

This book has been lovingly created by
a marvellous gang of good friends – writers,
illustrators, designers, engineers and,
believe it or not, angels.

We're on a mission to create as
many magical moments as possible for
grownups and children around the world.

Every book is made to order, just for you.

5367992

en-US